this book belongs to:

_____

PUBLISHED IN AUSTRALIA BY
WELDON KIDS PTY LTD
A MEMBER OF THE WELDON INTERNATIONAL GROUP OF COMPANIES

FIRST PUBLISHED 1995
REPRINT 1998, 1999, 2001, 2002, 2003, 2004, 2005, 2006, 2008

© WELDON KIDS PTY LTD

NATIONAL LIBRARY OF AUSTRALIA
CATALOGUING-IN-PUBLICATION DATA
FLEMING, GARRY, 1967 —
BOLLYGUM

ISBN 1 875875 06 9
ISBN 1 875875 08 5 (PBK)

I. TITLE.
A823.3

BOLLYGUM

Story and paintings by GARRY FLEMING

WELDON
KiDS

*All of us at Weldon Kids would like to dedicate this book to
each precious wild place and its preservation,
and to Garry's grandfather for believing in his dreams.*

Sunlight danced on the water and the trees swayed overhead . . .

Deep in the Australian bush there are hidden valleys where time has stood still. This is the story of one such place and the creatures that dwell there.

This is the story of Bollygum.

Sunlight filtered down through towering gum trees warming the darkest corners of the valley floor. The tiny community of Bollygum began to stir. Everyone, that is, except for wombat who had risen early and was busily getting ready for a day's fishing.

Wombat lived in a small house under the shadow of a tall ghost gum. Perfumes from his garden of orange passionflowers and pink boronias filled the air. He had spent the early hours of the morning carefully preparing his tackle box. Like everything in wombat's home, it was perfectly neat and well organised: only sinkers in the spot for sinkers, and only hooks in the spot for hooks.

"Yesterday I went fishing . . . ahh . . . the day before I went fishing . . . and . . . ahh . . . the day before that I went, ummm, fishing ... and yes, today looks like a perfect day for . . . ahh . . . fishing," muttered wombat. He gave a quick pat at the tuft of hair on the top of his head which, after a night spent squashed against his pillow, refused to lie down.

"Ready at last!" he said, and grabbed his best fishing rod, before heading down towards the creek.

After a short walk through the trees he came to his favourite fishing spot, a large rock that overlooked the deep, clear waters of the creek. Wriggling his rather round rump into a comfy position, he finally cast his line and watched as the sinker hit the surface of the water.

His float settled and the water smoothed. Wombat gave a contented sigh. Maybe this would be the day he actually caught something. He had never hooked a fish before, only watched as silvery shapes darted to and fro avoiding his hook. But wombat didn't mind; he enjoyed gazing at the tranquil creek and the stark white trunks of the tall ghost gums.

Sunlight danced on the water and the trees swayed overhead. Wombat sat and sat. As time slowly passed the warmth made him sleepy. Soon, very soon, it would be time to eat the delicious lunch he had so carefully packed in his tackle box.

Lunchtime came and went. Wombat wiped the crumbs away from his mouth and checked his line—just in case. He gazed along the bank of the creek at a crooked chimney that rose from a little red shingled roof. The small house could just be seen amongst the yellow wattle.

All the creatures of Bollygum knew it was platypus's home, but that was all they knew. Wombat had never been inside the house of the mysterious platypus, who was thought to be shy and eccentric. Like all the folk of Bollygum, wombat had only ever caught a fleeting glimpse of platypus's trailing tail as it disappeared around a corner on one of his rare visits to town. And although wombat visited the creek daily to fish, he wasn't brave enough to knock on platypus's door and introduce himself. Wombat wondered what platypus's life was like, how he spent his days and what lay within the walls of his house.

Suddenly, he was wide awake. "What was that!?" he said, as he searched some nearby ferns with wide eyes. "There it is again." He listened carefully. It was the faint sound of someone crying.

"Who . . . who's there?" whispered wombat, his voice shaking almost as much as his knees. He didn't like surprises, and had to force himself not to take off as fast as he could in the opposite direction.

"Who is it? What's the matter?" he called again, mustering up the courage that always seemed to leave him at the first hint of trouble. Taking a deep breath, he approached the ferns sprouting from the base of a large gum. Carefully parting the mass of green, he nervously peered between the fronds. The large, dark eyes of a little possum peered back at him.

"Oh dear, oh my," said wombat. "What's all the crying about?"

After some coaxing, the possum came into the light. Now wombat could see she was a tiny brush-tail possum. Feeling more relaxed, he took a red handkerchief from his pocket and caught a tear that was rolling down the little possum's cheek. She sniffed and another tear formed in the corner of her eye. Wombat offered his handkerchief again and put a comforting arm around her tiny, heaving shoulders.

"There, there," said wombat. "Wipe those tears away and tell me what's wrong. What is this all about?"

She sniffed again, and raised her big, dark eyes.

Little possum couldn't get the words out at first. Every time she tried to speak she choked on her own sobs. Finally, however, she managed to calm down enough to begin her story.

"I'm from the city and . . ."

"The city," gasped wombat. "I've never seen a city. I've heard they're big and noisy and there's, and there's—" he babbled, momentarily forgetting little possum's dilemma. Clearing his throat with a touch of embarrassment, he encouraged her to go on.

"I was trapped in the roof where my family lives, by a man with a big hessian sack. He packed me into the back of his car and drove me out of the city. We seemed to travel along a bumpy dirt road for a long way before he stopped and let me loose. I've been out all night trying to find my way back . . . I want to go home!"

At this she started sobbing all over again, dabbing her eyes once again with wombat's handkerchief. Wombat stood in front of her with his mouth wide open.

"The city and the road," he echoed. Again his mind began to wander. Everyone knew the dangers of 'the road'. If you went too close to the road there was a good chance you'd never come back. The rumblers might get you.

"Oh dear, oh my," said wombat. It was all too much for him. The only puzzle he had ever solved was deciding what to eat. This was much more serious. Aware that two pleading eyes were looking up at him, he rubbed his bristly chin and tried to look wise. He couldn't think what to do or say. Then, just as he was beginning to feel awkward, he spied platypus's chimney. Maybe platypus knew about the city!

"Come with me," he said, trying to sound more confident. "Perhaps platypus can help. And on the way you can tell me about the city."

Little possum began to feel more hopeful as they made their way along the edge of the creek to platypus's house. On the way she told him of her home high in the roof of a big house owned by the Raymond family. She spoke of the plentiful food and of the warmth from the fire the Raymonds burnt all winter long.

"Really, I don't understand why you would want to live anywhere but the city," she commented.

Wombat scratched his head as red-blue dragonflies skimmed across the waters. Well, it certainly sounded nice enough. He wouldn't mind seeing it for himself after what little possum had told him. But wombat didn't have time to think about it much longer, because they were outside platypus's front gate and now he was trying to look very brave.

He looked up, and suddenly he realised the walls were covered with paintings of all types of fish . . .

The splintered wooden gate hung loosely on its hinges near the water's edge. Nearby, tadpoles flickered between glistening tree roots that snaked their way into the creek.

Platypus's humble house, draped in native raspberry, looked a little run-down close up. The red roof was missing the odd shingle and the walls were faded.

"Someone lives here?" said little possum, thinking of the grand brick homes in the city where she lived. "And, if it's not a rude question, what exactly is a platypus?"

Wombat looked down at his small companion. "Oh yes, platypus lives here. He's not one for socialising, you see, so he doesn't really worry about what his house looks like. As for what he looks like himself, I can only tell you that he has a broad, flat tail."

Wombat was beginning to wonder if asking platypus for help was a good idea. But he had come this far, so he felt he might as well knock on the door. Pushing the gate open, he walked softly up to the front door and gave it a light tap. It swung open. Wombat leapt back. Gathering himself together quickly before little possum could see how nervous he was he called, "Platypus, are you home?"

There was no answer. He tried again. No answer. With little possum now beside him, wombat stepped up to the door and poked his head in.

"Platypus?" Nothing.

They looked all around the big room that platypus called home. It seemed as though platypus had collected every bit of old furniture thrown out by the creatures of Bollygum. There were old pots and pans hanging from a mantel-piece, dusty leather-bound books, odd-shaped jars in many colours and chairs of all kinds. The piles reached the ceiling in some places.

Amid all the clutter was an artist's easel. The sun poured through a window and lit up the brightly painted canvas. It was too tempting for wombat. He had to get closer to the painting to see what it was. With little possum following, he crossed the room and stood in front of the canvas.

"Oh me, oh my!" Wombat couldn't believe his eyes. It was the most wonderful painting he had ever seen—of a fish! He looked up, and suddenly he realised the walls were covered with paintings of all types of fish. It was like being in the middle of a stream and watching the fish swim past in flashes of colour. He turned around and around taking in all the glorious scenes.

It was on his third time round that he stopped dead. There in the sunlit doorway was the strangest creature he had ever seen.

Wombat gulped.

As the creature began to come into focus he could make out a furry body, a bill and webbed feet that seemed to belong to a duck, and a tail that looked as if it had been ironed once too often. Behind wombat, little possum stifled a giggle.

"Terribly sorry for barging in like this, Mr Platypus," stuttered wombat. "We thought you were in."

Platypus took a few paces forward. Over his shoulder he had a haul of fish, which he slung down on the table with a loud THWAP. Wombat's eyes widened.

Platypus was silent, gesturing for them to take a seat. Wombat introduced little possum, and told about her being lost and needing to get back to the city and her family.

"I thought maybe you could help us," wombat said, his eyes still fixed on the impressive catch.

There was silence. Wombat held his breath anxious to hear the creature speak. Platypus hung his hat behind the door. Everything about him seemed slow, almost awkward.

"I'm sorry, but I don't think I can be of much help. I'm afraid I know nothing of this place you call the city. The only advice I can offer you is to call a town meeting. There may be someone else in Bollygum who will be able to help."

Although you could hardly call him chatty, he seems like a decent sort of fellow, thought wombat. And those marvellous paintings!

"Yes, well thank you," he said. "That's just what we'll do. We'll call a town meeting. Thank you again for your advice. We'd better get along then."

Before they left, platypus pressed a bag into wombat's paw.

"Lily-pad biscuits, baked them fresh this morning," he explained. Wombat and little possum thanked him once more and started on their way back to Bollygum. After a while, little possum turned to wombat, who was happily munching on a biscuit.

"He's not like anything I've ever imagined!" she said, and they both chuckled.

A few twists and turns later, they reached the path that led into Bollygum, and made their way to the meeting place. Picking up a large stick, wombat gave a huge hollow gum three big raps. Deep loud hums echoed down through the valley. Wombat clambered onto an old stump and lifted little possum up beside him.

The meeting had been called!

Before long most of the creatures of Bollygum had gathered in front of the meeting stump. There, amongst the crowd, were ring-tail possum and echidna and goanna. Not forgetting kookaburra and, arriving in a rush, the disagreeable frilled lizard.

From her perch, little possum could see the town over their heads. She had to admit it was rather delightful. The smell of fresh-baked bread wafted through the air, no highrise buildings blocked out the sun, no cars roared down streets. Flowers bloomed everywhere, cicadas droned in the grass and small birds chattered in the trees. It certainly was a long way from the city!

Lowering her gaze to the town's inhabitants, little possum realised that platypus didn't look so strange after all. There amongst the crowd was a lizard that seemed to have swallowed an open umbrella. What an odd lot! she thought.

Folding his muscular arms over his ample belly, Goanna tapped his foot impatiently.

"Well, womppbat?" he spluttered, his tongue whipping about comically. "Whappt's thipps all about? And who ipps your friend?"

Wombat felt nervous in front of the large crowd, he cleared his throat. "I, err, would like you all to meet, ahh, our little visitor. She has, umm, a problem we must to try to help her with."

"HAA HAA HAA . . . and what might that problem be? HOO HOO HOO . . . oops! Sorry," cackled kookaburra, clamping a wing over his beak. He was never able to say anything, no matter how serious, without laughing.

Wombat was aware everyone was looking straight at him. "The problem? Oh, it's . . . umm. Oh dear, oh my! I forget."

At that point ring-tail possum, one of the town leaders, leapt on to the stump.

"Perhaps little possum could tell us what the problem is," he suggested. And she did just that.

When she had finished there was a heavy silence. Then came a loud, "TUT!"

"The city?" cried frilled lizard. "Yuk, horrible place. Oh no, no, no. Can't help you there, it's just too hard. Why, there . . ." A harsh glare from ring-tail possum stopped him in his tracks.

"Anybody with anything useful to say?" asked ring-tail. A tiny voice answered.

"Cockatoo might know about the city," said echidna softly. "She might visit it on her flights." Echidna didn't often speak, but when she did it generally made sense.

"Whappt a good idea!" spluttered goanna. "But how do we find her?"

He was considered quite a wizard, his magic well respected by most . . .

At that instant there was a commotion at the back of the crowd. Little possum could see a blue hat jostling its way to the front. It was frogmouth.

"What's all this fuss, and how can you conduct a meeting without my presence?" he blurted, waving his hands. Frogmouth lived at the top end of town. He only ever came outdoors to voice his opinion or to be nosey. He always wore an impressive wizard's gown and matching blue hat. It wasn't unusual to see puffs of smoke or hear loud bangs coming from frogmouth's house as he dabbled in his magic behind closed doors. He was considered quite a wizard and his magic well respected by most.

Everything was retold for frogmouth's benefit. He closed his eyes and nodded his head. The crowd waited.

"I'll call on cockatoo with my magic powers," said frogmouth excitedly. "Yes, I'll summon him by way of great magic. Hurry to my place." He straightened up his hat and puffed out his chest proudly.

And so before ring-tail could get another word in, frogmouth turned and strutted off in the direction of his house, with all in tow.

As the excited crowd rolled towards frogmouth's house, ring-tail's memory began to tug at him. He had always been doubtful about frogmouth's magic and, on checking his watch, he allowed himself a knowing smile. It was almost 2 o'clock and, on most days, that was when cockatoo arrived to lunch on her favourite tree in Bollygum. So that's what frogmouth was up to!

But there was another, more important, memory pricking at his mind. Just as the crowd reached frogmouth's front door he snapped his fingers and raced off, headed for home. No-one noticed he was missing, they were so thrilled by the chance to see frogmouth's magic.

Once inside, frogmouth went straight to a large book spread open on a table in the centre of the room.

Little possum had thought that platypus's home was the most curious she would ever see, but this was even more bizarre. It must truly be the home of a master magician!

While frogmouth flicked through the pages of his book, little possum gawped at the amazing collection of weird and wonderful objects that filled the room.

> *There were piles of books on piles of books,*
> *Strange things hung on twisted hooks,*
> *Shelves were cluttered with bottles and pots,*
> *Colours and crannies and splashes and spots.*
> *Spiderwebs draped off knobs and handles,*
> *Shadows were cast by burning candles.*

Frogmouth finally found what he'd been looking for and jabbed his wingtip at the page.

"Ah hah! Here it is," he exclaimed.

The crowd strained forward to have a look, and he shooed them back. He then placed a wooden bowl in front of him, took down a magic bottlebrush branch from a shelf and closed his big, orange eyes. The crowd went very, very quiet.

Frogmouth raised the branch above his head and began to chant a spell. His other wing whooshed and swished through the air in time with his mumbled words. Minutes passed.

Frogmouth's wing flapped wildly, and nobody else moved a muscle.

Then, as the crowd stared at the magic bottlebrush, frogmouth half-opened an eye to peek at the clock above the doorway. It was almost on the stroke of 2 o'clock.

Closing his eyes tightly again, Frogmouth reached into the folds of his gown and lifted out some reddish powder. With a loud "Cockatoo!" that startled the crowd, he tossed the powder into the bowl and it erupted in a cloud of pink smoke.

Before the smoke had disappeared they heard it —the coarse screech of cockatoo sounding down the valley. Then the screech was almost drowned out by the chorus of "oohs" and "aahs" that came from the astonished crowd.

Frogmouth wiped his brow and puffed out his chest. Everywhere he turned there were admiring looks. No-one would ever doubt his magic powers now! And he eagerly prepared to accept their congratulations.

But before he could receive even his first pat on the back, ring-tail came bursting through the door clutching a scroll of paper.

"I've found it!" he cried excitedly. "I've found it!"

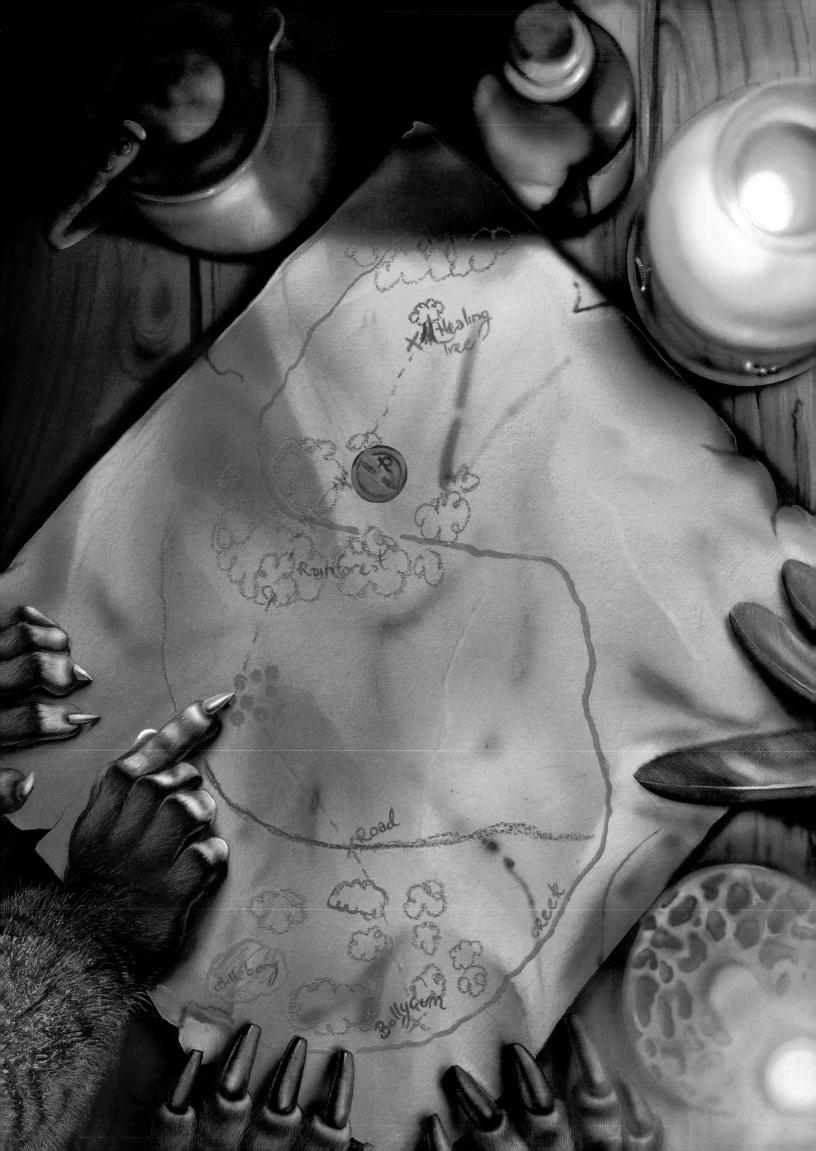

Ring-tail marched to the table, pushed the bowl aside and spread the scroll out.

"It's a map!" cried wombat as the crowd gathered about the table.

"It's a map all right, and it's marked from Bollygum, right to the edge of the city," said ring-tail, running his finger across the tattered paper.

"I remember my grandfather showing it to me when I was young. He talked about a journey he had taken in search of a rare plant. A plant that was needed to heal a very sick baby."

"Did he find the plant?" they all asked.

"Yes, he found it all right. I wouldn't be here if he didn't. Five days north from here, right at the edge of the city. He drew this map along the way, and it seems fairly well marked. It will take us right to the end of the bush, and from there little possum should be able to find her way home," he said, patting her on the shoulder.

The cheers almost lifted the roof off frog-mouth's home. Little possum just beamed, lost for words.

"And who do you propose is going to take her there?" grunted frilled lizard.

"I will," said ring-tail. " . . . my grandfather— I'll do it for him, he'd be proud of that, but I'm going to need two volunteers. It's a long way there and back, and it's bound to be dangerous. Who will join us?"

Wombat looked around for a moment, took a big breath and stepped forward.

"I will," he said, trying to hide the trace of fear in his voice. "I'll take you home, little possum."

Little possum smiled up at her friend and threw her arms around his broad middle and hugged him. At the same time, goanna stepped forward.

"I don't mind a bippt of adventure myself," he declared. "I'd like to see whappt thipps city ipps all about. Mayppbe I'd like to live there too."

Ring-tail surveyed his fellow adventurers. They'd make an unlikely looking bunch, he thought, but he was confident they could do the job.

"Now, there's no reason we can't get started this afternoon," he said. "We just need everyone to organise supplies while I go and see whether cockatoo will join us. You never know, we might need some help from the air at some stage."

Not wanting to waste time, ring-tail quickly rolled up the map and went to find cockatoo. Wombat, goanna and little possum left to get ready. Frogmouth swallowed his disappointment at having his big moment taken over and started issuing orders to the remaining trio.

"Kookaburra, frilled lizard and echidna, go off as fast as you can and gather something to eat and drink."

"What?" complained frilled lizard. Frogmouth silenced him with a mouth full of feathers and then announced that everyone was to be at the meeting place in an hour.

The great adventure was about to begin!

Ring-tail had no trouble finding cockatoo. She was chewing away on the seeds of her favourite acacia tree. Jumping out of the way of the falling husks, he called out to her and asked her to come down. With a raucous screech she flew off the branch, circled once and landed at his feet.

Cockatoo listened patiently to the whole story, her sulphur-crest raised at attention. It turned out that although she had only ever flown close to the city, she was more than willing to help.

"Cockatoo's flying guide at your service, ring-tail!" she squawked, almost splitting his ears at such close range. Ring-tail, his ears ringing, thanked her and explained that they would be leaving that afternoon. Could she meet them as soon as she'd finished lunch, please? And would she just nod, if it was okay?

Now ring-tail returned to his home to ready himself for what he knew would be the trip of a lifetime. His heart beat faster at the thought of leaving Bollygum behind, even for a short while. But the more he thought about it, the more excited he became. He would be travelling in his grandfather's footsteps and actually seeing the tree that had saved his life.

It was with pride in his step that ring-tail arrived at the meeting stump. The others were already there, chattering loudly and comparing each other's offerings for the journey.

Wombat had brought some banksia buns,
Echidna a pot of stew,
From kookaburra the gumnut juice
Honey from cockatoo,
Frogmouth showed with wattle scones,
Frilled lizard plain forgot,
Votes were cast before they left:
Goanna to carry the lot!

The time had come to say farewell. Little possum thanked everybody for their help, and wombat tried to look as brave as possible. Finally, as the trees's shadows spread further across the town, the small party waved goodbye and began the walk out of the valley.

They tramped along through the late afternoon hours, each lost in their own thoughts. Cockatoo flew lazily overhead. The sun was well below the treeline when they reached the top of the valley, the edge of the known world for the creatures of Bollygum. As they gazed back on their beloved home, their stomachs knotted. It seemed, for a moment, like the most beautiful place in the world. Evening bird calls filtered up from below and a burning pink sky painted the scene in soft light. Even little possum found herself wishing she could stay a while longer.

Ring-tail's words floated up towards the stars and were carried away by a tender breeze . . .

Darkness came quickly. The first stars were beginning to sparkle when they agreed to camp for the night.

Wombat and cockatoo gathered twigs to light a fire while goanna laid out the supplies and ring-tail built a fireplace from rocks. Before long they were eating their banksia buns by a blazing fire. Great white moths, attracted by the light, danced above the flames.

When dinner had been eaten and washed down with gumnut juice, ring-tail unfurled the map and studied it by the firelight. After some moments he put it down and scratched his stomach, something he always did when he was deep in thought.

"According to this," said ring-tail, "we'll have to cross the road first thing in the morning."

Wombat shuddered.

"Is there anything you can tell us about it?" ring-tail asked little possum.

"Well, I guess it's the same with all roads," she said. "My mother always says not to look into the bright eyes of the cars—you call them rumblers, I think—or you risk your life. Never, ever look into their eyes!"

The others nodded. Wombat felt a shiver run down his spine. Goanna finally broke the silence.

"I think I'll geppt some sleep. We've goppt a long way to go and we'll need plenty of reppst."

It was just the signal the others were waiting for. Cockatoo flapped her wings and took roost in a low branch. Underneath, the four weary adventurers bedded down in the soft earth. Lying back, little possum suddenly pointed to the twinkling sky.

"I've never seen so many stars!" she exclaimed. "And they're so bright!"

"Yes, and see over there, that's the Southern Cross," said ring-tail. "We sleep under her every night."

With some prodding, they encouraged little possum to talk about life in the city.

To the little band of Bollygum creatures it all seemed very strange. When little possum finished, ring-tail scanned the night sky. Bats scudded between treetops, their velvet wings making soothing music in the air.

"Our world doesn't seem to change as fast as yours. Everything only changes as fast as things grow or as each season passes. And these changes are gentle ones and ones we have a knowledge of from the generations before us," said ring-tail.

Ring-tail's words floated up towards the stars and were carried away by a tender breeze. The same breeze that lulled them to sleep on their first night beyond Bollygum.

Daybreak arrived with a chorus from sweet-voiced birds. Crimson rosellas fed noisily on the blossoms of a nearby tree as the group enjoyed a breakfast of honey and scones in the watery early light.

Soon ring-tail was leading them on their way. They had barely stretched their legs, however, when their leader came to a sudden halt. They crowded forward to look over his shoulder.

It was the road. A dusty stretch of red earth. As they peered left and right in the gloom they could just make out sharp bends in both directions. Wombat's heart was pounding so hard against his chest he thought it might burst!

"Cockatoo," called ring-tail, "is there anything coming?"

"Nothing that I can see," she squawked from above, squinting into the patches of darkness.

"Thappt's it," said goanna. "Leppt's go!"

And with a mad scamper goanna was across the road. Ring-tail and little possum skipped across to join him. When they turned, wombat was still on the other side.

"Come on, wombat!" they shouted.

Wombat looked across at them, looked down the road once more and, with a racing heart, put his paw on the road. He began waddling across in his fastest wombat way. Until, half-way over, he suddenly stopped. His eyes grew large (for a wombat) and he began to tremble.

"Can you feel it?" he whispered loudly.

They could. A tingling feeling under their feet. cockatoo screeched something from overhead.

"It's a rumbler!" cried ring-tail. "Hurry, wombat, hurry!"

At that moment a terrifying sight came into view around the corner. A huge metallic beast with blazing eyes, chewing up the road in a cloud of dust.

"Don't look into the eyes!" shouted little possum, but wombat was already staring dumbly at the fiery headlights. It was too late.

The car was almost on wombat when goanna threw off his backpack and leapt across the road. A second later the huge wheels rumbled past and churned up a choking dust cloud before disappearing around another corner. Ring-tail, wiping the dust from his eyes, ran into the middle of the road.

"Wombat! Goanna! Where are you?" he called.

There was no reply. Ring-tail held little possum's face against his belly.

A splutter came from the other side of the road. Ring-tail swung around, raced over and looked in a ditch. It was filled with a great tangle of limbs.

"Wombat! Goanna! You're alive!"

Wombat looked up. "I think the rumbler hit me," he said in a surprised tone.

"Ippt was me who hippt you!" said a muffled voice beneath him. Wombat rolled over and looked in wonder at goanna.

"Sorry, sorry, goanna. How ever can I thank you?"

Goanna dusted himself off and shrugged. By now everyone had gathered around him with admiring looks.

"Ippt's nothing, Womppbat," said Goanna, feeling very much the hero. "Just make sure I land on top next time!"

All about them was the most glorious forest of flowers . . .

Leaving the road behind them, the group continued north. They tramped along ridges, dropped into gullies and weaved in and out of thick trees. Every so often they would stop and study the map to make sure they were heading in the right direction. The signposts were in the land itself—a ravine here, a hilltop there, a stream to the left, a clump of trees to the right.

There was one sign that puzzled everyone, however. They moved on, heads swivelling to and fro in search of the mysterious red dots.

And as they went, little possum marvelled at the beauty all around. One minute they passed a rippling creek, the waters gurgling between smooth rocks. The next they would be softly stroked by a field of flannel flowers. All the while wings beat the air as birds with wonderful names like honeyeater, fantail and golden whistler (so ring-tail told her) went in search of food. Of course, she had seen some of these birds in the city. But they seemed so out of place there, and no-one really cared about their names.

Just as little possum was watching a blue-tongued lizard sunning itself on a rock, there came a screech from above.

"The red dots! The red dots!" screeched cockatoo.

They looked up. And up, and up. Thick stems soared into the sky, where huge red waratahs flowered in a burst of colour. All about them was the most glorious forest of flowers they had ever seen!

"They're so beautiful!" cried wombat.

"Oh, what a wonderful, wonderful place!" cried little possum, throwing her paws in the air and skipping in circles.

As they gazed up in open-mouthed wonder, honeyeaters and spinebills dipped their beaks into the flowers. The adventurers stood there for what seemed like hours, sprays of red pollen falling on their heads as the birds flitted from flower to flower.

In the end, ring-tail had to remind everybody of the journey still ahead. Sadly, they agreed to start moving again, and they were soon climbing a steep bank. At the top, before the waratahs were out of view, little possum turned to take a last look at the sea of red below. It was a sight she would never forget.

They travelled late into the afternoon, reaching a winding stream at the edge of the rainforest before dusk. Goanna, rubbing his tired feet, suggested this was a good place to camp for the night, and everyone quickly agreed. A fire was made and echidna's stew was gratefully eaten. The exhausted group made their beds under trees painted silver by a great yellow moon.

Little possum drifted off to sleep with a broad smile on her face.

The crack of a whipbird call greeted first light. After a quick breakfast ring-tail led the way across a shallow stream to the fringe of the rainforest.

With that, they stepped through the dense green curtain and into a soft and dimly lit world. There were patches of rainforest in Bollygum, but none as vast as this one. Giant tree trunks flowed up from the ground, moss blanketed the forest floor and palms and vines dropped over the path. Glowing green butterflies hovered between the branches. High above ferns clung to the trees and sunlight struggled to pierce the dense leaves.

Goanna headed the group, muscling his way through the thick foliage for hour after hour. At the back wombat wiped the sweat from his brow.

"It's steamy in here, isn't it?" panted wombat. But nobody had the breath to answer. Then, as they rounded a particularly big tree, wombat found himself gazing at the most extraordinary orchid. He dropped to his knees to look closely at its bright red and yellow patterns and then thrust his large nose into its centre to sniff the sweet fragrance.

By the time he turned around there was no sign of the others.

"Ring-tail? Goanna?" he called. But they were nowhere to be seen.

He was not scared at first. He hurried ahead, calling as he went. Then as the minutes passed he became more anxious, and tried to move even quicker. But the faster he tried to go the more he tripped over vines and logs.

Deeper and deeper he went into the forest. Sweat began to run in streams off his nose. As he looked all about, the fungis seemed to wink at him and the trees seemed to sneer. He called louder and louder, but still there was no reply. In a panic he began to run, crashing into trees and getting tangled in vines.

"Ring-tail? Goanna? Where are you?"

A faint call answered. Wombat stopped, listened again, and followed the sound.

"Wombat! We though we'd lost you!"

Wombat couldn't hide his relief. He raced up to his friends, only to be stopped by a sudden howl of laughter.

"What have you done, Wombat?" cried little possum, pointing straight at him.

Wombat looked down and shrieked. He was covered, head to foot, in a bright red rash.

"Oh dear, oh my, what is it? And my goodness it burns and itches," he said.

"It looks like you've had a run-in with a stinging tree," said ring-tail, trying not to laugh. "Don't worry. We'll go back and find it. The calla lily always grows right next to them and the juice is the cure."

"You do look awful," screeched cockatoo, as they all followed ring-tail back through the trees. The forest echoed with wombat's "ouchs" . . . and little possum's giggles.

No matter how much he wiggled and squirmed, wombat was firmly wedged in . . .

After rubbing calla lily juice all over wombat to stop the stinging, they all sat down for a bite to eat. That is, everyone but wombat, who was dancing about with relief.

"You are a wonder, ring-tail, a real wonder, my friend," he said.

"We may as well camp here for the night," ring-tail said. Night was coming early in this half-light world as ring-tail spread the map out and peered at his grandfather's markings.

"We still have to cross quite a wide creek before we get through the rainforest. We'll know when we're almost out when we reach something that my grandfather's marked as a blue button. Goodness knows what that is."

The morning of the fourth day saw them trekking through the rainforest, wombat keeping one eye out for stinging trees and the other on his friends. Towards lunchtime they found themselves pushing through lush pockets of ferns to a fast-swirling creek lined with great lilies. The water was too deep to cross, but they could see a fallen tree spanning the creek further along.

"It's awfully slippery," said little possum when they reached the log.

Goanna crouched and smiled. "Pippin's hollow," he announced. "I can see lighppt appt the other end."

The others peered into the log. Goanna was right.

"Yes, yes, we'll go through it," said wombat, very relieved at not having to test his balance on the mossy bridge.

So ring-tail poked his head in the log and began to crawl to the other side. It was slow going, but he soon popped out on the opposite bank, wiping the dirt from his knees. Little possum was next, and she quickly joined ring-tail on the other side of the creek. Next came wombat. In he went and, after some thumping and bumping, out came his head on the other side. Then his shoulders. Then . . .

"I'm stuck!" wailed wombat. "My bottom's too big!"

No matter how much he wiggled and squirmed, wombat was firmly wedged in—unable to go forward or backwards. Finally, ring-tail and little possum took hold of an arm each and yanked. And yanked. And yanked. It was no good. Wombat didn't budge an inch!

"Whappt's the hold-upp?" came goanna's muffled voice from within the log.

"Wombat's stuck," shouted ring-tail. "Can you try to push him out from your side?"

Goanna snorted, and put his shoulder to wombat's backside. He pushed and he shoved and he pressed. But still wombat couldn't be moved.

"Oh dear, oh my," puffed wombat. All was quiet.

Suddenly there was a loud "SNAP!" from inside the log and, with a great bellow, wombat came hurtling out of the log.

Ring-tail rushed over to his friend. "What happened? What's the matter?"

Wombat just sat there, rubbing his bottom. But ring-tail's question was answered when goanna emerged from the log.

"Leppt's move on, shall we?" smirked goanna, removing a small shred of wombat's overalls from his mouth.

Goanna led the group through the afternoon. As they neared the edge of the rainforest ring-tail began to wonder if they were still on course. He was so lost in thought about the meaning of the blue button that he jumped when a satin bower bird suddenly appeared in front of them.

"Whee-ooo, what have we here?" asked bower bird. "And why have you entered my bower?"

"We're on our way to the city," explained ring-tail. "To take little possum back to her family. As for entering your bower, I don't even know what a bower is."

Bower bird sniffed. "Why, it's my home. My castle. And you're standing in it!"

They looked around, and realised they were standing on a layer of sticks and twigs. Next to them, two great stick-walls arched high above their heads. They were decorated with blue and yellow-green feathers, flowers, berries and shells.

"We . . . hadn't realised . . . this was your home," said ring-tail.

Wombat had noticed a pile of blue stones and shells that his curiosity couldn't resist. "Oh, they're lovely," he gasped, rushing to them.

"Don't touch," cried bower bird, as wombat reached to pick some up. "It took me hours to arrange," he wailed, brushing wombat away with a wave of his hand.

"Why do you have so many beautiful blue things?" asked little possum.

"I'm a satin bower bird, and satin bower birds collect blue things. I love blue, anything blue, oh just give me blue, blue, blue," he cried, twirling.

Bower bird was suddenly knocked off his feet as ring-tail dived in and scattered his neat pile. "That's it!" he exclaimed, grasping something tightly in his fist. "The blue button look, it's identical to the one on grandfather's map!"

"Just a minute," interrupted bower bird, leaping to his feet. "That's private property."

"Please, sir," said ring-tail humbly, realising his rudeness, "how did you acquire it?"

"Let me see," began bower bird. He scratched his head for a moment. "Ah, I remember. A traveller gave it to me long ago. Yes, I gave him directions and he gave me that blue button in return. In fact, now I think of him, he looked a little like you!"

"That's because he was my grandfather," smiled ring-tail. "May I keep it, bower bird?" he asked, rubbing the button between his fingers.

"Definitely not!" replied bower bird sternly. "It's mine."

"Now just a minute," screeched cockatoo.

But it was little possum who stepped forward. "I have this," she said, producing a hair clip from her pocket. A bright blue hair clip. Bower bird's eyes lit up with excitement. He let out an appreciative, "Oh, it's beautiful."

"I'll trade you," said little possum. "The clip for the button."

So ring-tail got his grandfather's button and they quickly went on their way. Little possum looked over her shoulder and smiled. Bower bird was strutting up and down in front of his bower, proudly showing off his newly acquired blue hair clip, pinned firmly upon his chest.

Millions of stars seemed to have fallen from the sky to land on the Earth far below . . .

As the afternoon wore on the travellers climbed higher and higher, until they found themselves at the top of a waterfall. Looking down, they could see the water slapping against rocks below before it broke into little pools and trickled to the bottom. It seemed like a good place to cool their feet and have another look at the map.

"We can follow this ridge for the rest of the afternoon and camp beside these falls," said ring-tail, pointing to the map. "If we follow the falls down, the creek will take us right to the healing tree and the edge of the city. We should be there by early tomorrow afternoon."

They all nodded. After having a snack and drinking from the clear water, they picked themselves up and began to follow the ridge. The cloudless sky turned from seashell pink to a dark blue washed with rose as they neared their campsite, ring-tail leading the way.

The cry stopped everyone in their tracks. Up ahead ring-tail stood beside the waterfall, swaying from side to side.

"Oh no!" he cried. "Oh no!"

They raced up to join him as cockatoo landed at his side. One by one they stopped and gasped at the sight that lay beneath them. Millions of stars seemed to have fallen from the sky to land on the Earth far below. It was the lights of the city!

Giant buildings crowded into the evening air. Rumblers roared along paved roads. As far as the eye could see the city spread itself over the land. Where were the trees? The birds? The flowers?

Ring-tail slowly unrolled the map.

"But we have only travelled four days," he said quietly. "The healing tree, the creek, it's all gone."

Wombat patted his friend on the shoulder. But there was nothing he could say. He had no words to describe what he saw below. It was so much bigger and noisier than he had ever imagined. He couldn't hear the birds' evening songs at all. And it was so hungry—hadn't it eaten up the healing tree and the creek since ring-tail's grandfather had visited?

Little possum, too, was lost for words. Suddenly the city didn't seem like such a wonderful place after all. She thought about the fire-red waratahs, the cool, clear streams, the towering rainforest trees and the nights spent under a blanket of brilliant stars. She remembered the butterflies and the scent of wildflowers. She remembered Bollygum.

A tear rolled down little possum's cheek.

Minutes passed before goanna broke the silence. Ring-tail was now sitting glumly on a rock, his head bowed.

"Ippt's getting dark, little possum," said goanna. "If you want to make ippt back to your family tonighppt, you had better leave soon. They muppst be terribly worried about you. Can you see your home from here?"

They all turned to their little friend. She was wiping her eyes with the red handkerchief wombat had given her in Bollygum.

"Yes, it's next to that clocktower you can see over there," said little possum in a small voice. She pointed into the distance where they could see a large clockface under a tilting roof.

The time had come to say goodbye. Cockatoo opened her broad, white wings and gave little possum a smothering hug.

"You must come and visit one day, cockatoo," said little possum. "We have one of your favourite acacia trees growing in our front yard."

Cockatoo squawked her thanks.

Next, goanna and a glassy-eyed ring-tail gave little possum a fond squeeze.

"I'll miss you both very much," said little possum, trying to hold back the tears. "Thank you for all you've done."

Then she faced wombat. He was staring at the ground, shuffling his feet. As he looked up with dewy eyes she stepped forward and pressed her cheek to his soft belly.

"I'll never forget you," whispered little possum.

Wombat hugged her tight as the tears flowed down their faces. Little possum tried to catch her tears in the handkerchief and then offered it to wombat.

"No, you keep it," sniffed wombat. "Whenever you use it you can think of us."

"I'll miss you all," said little possum. And with a final look over her shoulder she disappeared down the slope.

It was ring-tail who broke the silence this time.

"Come on, everyone. We'll move a little way back before we camp tonight. I can't stay here any longer. It will only make me sadder."

They all agreed and turned back along the ridge. The fire that night threw shadows on some very long faces. And for the whole journey home hardly a word was spoken. Everyone was lost in their own thoughts about the city and what it might mean for Bollygum. Wombat was also missing his little friend. Oh, how he would have liked to teach her how to fish!

But little possum was back with her family now. In the city. And Bollygum would never seem quite the same.

It was the biggest party Bollygum had ever seen . . .

When the adventurers returned to Bollygum the whole town turned up to hear the story of their journey. What had they seen? Was it dangerous outside the valley? Did little possum get home safely? What was the city like?

The creatures of Bollygum were entertained for many days and nights with tales of the road and the rainforest and wombat's misfortunes. The adventurers talked of the lights and the rumblers and the buildings that spread like a blanket across the land. From time to time, in the cool of evening, wombat, ring-tail and goanna would go for walks and sit by the creek to discuss their trip. Wombat would talk about their adventure, and they would enjoy again the times they had shared.

It was on one such evening that they sat and made their own map, just as ring-tail's grandfather had done before them, all hoping it would be the only update ever needed.

Since returning they had discovered fresh delight in the things they had once taken for granted in Bollygum. They often danced a little dance at the sight, sound and smell of the bush—the strong trees, the crystal waters, the sing-song birds and the perfumed flowers. At night wombat would say a prayer that it would all stay that way.

One of wombat's prayers, at least, was answered on a mild autumn day.

Wombat had just finished patting down the troublesome tuft of hair on his head and stepped outside to see whether it was a good day for fishing. He was looking up into the cloud-flecked sky when he saw cockatoo fly overhead. There was a loud screech and something dropped out of cockatoo's mouth. Something red. It floated down and landed at wombat's feet.

His red handkerchief!

He swung around to look up the path. Coming out of the trees, with two bigger possums behind, was little possum! Wombat let out a cry of delight. Little possum had followed Cockatoo from the city.

"Hello, wombat," squealed little possum. "I'm back! This is my family, and we're here to stay!"

It was the happiest day in wombat's life. After almost hugging the breath out of little possum, he rushed down to the meeting stump and struck it three times. An excited crowd gathered and heard about little possum's return. The cheers could be heard across the valley. And that night they held the biggest party Bollygum had ever seen.

Some say even platypus was there!

Around Bollygum, the wild, wide land
Is tranquil, untouched, ancient, grand—
A magic world of myth and story.
But real places share its glory:
Tasmania's Tarkine too abounds
In landscapes quiet and joyous sounds
Of creatures never seen elsewhere,
And plants and places all too rare.
Yet blows dealt by the human hand
With fire and fence and mine and mess
Unbalance things that proudly stand,
Conspire to makes the treasures less.
This book is for the Tarkine, and
All precious, fragile wilderness.

The Tarkine wilderness area, in the north-west corner of Tasmania, is rich in unusual animals, fragile plant life, coastal dunes, moorlands, river gores, caves, rainforest, mountains and unique Aboriginal sites. All of which will be lost unless it is declared a World Heritage Area.

PUBLISHING DIRECTOR: Leonie Weldon

MANAGING EDITOR: Ian Cockerill

EDITORIAL CONSULTANTS: Susan Scobie & Avril Janks

PROJECT & PROMOTIONS MANAGER: Leah Walsh

PRODUCTION MANAGER: Cath Wadling and Kirsty Partridge

DESIGNER: Astri Baker

PRINTED IN CHINA THROUGH: Jade Productions

WELDON
K*i*DS